cloverleaf books™

Alike and Different

My Religion, Your Religion

Lisa Bullard

illustrated by **Holli Conger**

Ⓜ MILLBROOK PRESS · MINNEAPOLIS

For Grandma B. —L.B.

For C.C. —H.C.

Millbrook Press
A division of Lerner Publishing Group, Inc.
241 First Avenue North
Minneapolis, MN 55401 USA

For reading levels and more information, look up this title at
www.lernerbooks.com.

Main body text set in Slappy Inline 18/28.
Typeface provided by T26.

Library of Congress Cataloging-in-Publication Data

Bullard, Lisa, author.
    My religion, your religion / By Lisa Bullard ; illustrated by
  Holli Conger.
        pages   cm. — (Cloverleaf books™. Alike and different)
      Audience: Ages 5–8.
      Includes bibliographical references and index.
      ISBN 978-1-4677-4905-3 (lib. bdg. : alk. paper)
      ISBN 978-1-4677-6033-1 (pbk.)
      ISBN 978-1-4677-6296-0 (EB pdf)
      1. Religions—Juvenile literature. I. Conger, Holli, illustrator.
    II. Title.
    BL92.B84 2015
    200—dc23   2014021272

Manufactured in the United States of America
1 – BP – 12/31/14

TABLE OF CONTENTS

Chapter One

A Special Invitation

Hi! I'm David. This is my neighbor Zach. He just turned thirteen. Zach is really nice for a big kid. **He teaches me about baseball.**

Zach invited me to a service at his synagogue. Dad explained that's where Jewish people worship. He's coming with me.

"I've never been to a synagogue," I remind Dad. **"What if I don't understand things?** What if I do something wrong?"

You're Invited

"Don't worry," Dad says. "We don't need to understand everything. **We just need to show respect.**" We go online to learn about being respectful at the synagogue.

We find out that thirteen is an important birthday for Jewish boys. The special service is Zach's bar mitzvah.

In Zach's religion, he is now an adult.

Jewish girls have a bat mitzvah. It is similar to a bar mitzvah for boys. Does your religion or family have special ways of celebrating young people?

When we get to the service, we're given a little cap to wear. It's called a **kippah**. I notice that other men and boys and some of the women and the girls are wearing them too.

It's fun to be part of Zach's special day! There are prayers and singing. I'm used to that from our church. Zach also reads in front of everyone. It's a language I don't know. Dad says it is **Hebrew.**

Chapter Two
Different Families, Different Beliefs

Sunday morning, Dad and I go to church. I look at the sign. "Is our religion called Lutheran?" I ask.

"It's called Christianity," he says. "There are different kinds of Christian churches. Lutheran is one kind. You and Mom go to a Catholic church. That's Christian too."

Many different religions can be found around the world. Does your family practice a religion?

I wonder why there are different kinds of churches. Do you think it's like fans choosing to follow different baseball teams?

I like going to both
my churches.

I get to see friends. I feel like
God listens while we pray.

I ask Dad if people of all religions pray. That would be a lot for God to listen to! "Not all religions have God as we think of God," says Dad.

"But people from many religions pray."

Different religions have different ways of praying. Does your family pray?

On Sunday afternoon, people from my church volunteer. **We help at a place that serves food to people who need it.** I see Sophia, my friend from school. She's volunteering too.

I ask Sophia if she's there with another church. She says her family isn't part of a religion.
They just like helping others.

15

Chapter Three

Many Religions

On the way home, I see lots of people in the park. "Remember Fahmi from my baseball team?" I ask Dad. "He told me his family is going to a big celebration here today. **Do you know what they're celebrating?**"

Dad tells me the month of **Ramadan** just ended for Muslims.

"But the month isn't over yet!" I say.

"Ramadan is part of their religious calendar," Dad says. "It's an important time for Muslims. When Ramadan is over, Muslims give thanks and celebrate. **It's called Eid al-Fitr.**"

Muslims call their god Allah. Ramadan is a special time for Muslims to get closer to Allah. Are there times of year that are special in your religion?

Later, Kate comes over to babysit. "I've been finding out about different religions," I tell her. "And Dad says there are even more."

"I've been studying Buddhism," Kate says. She tells me she's been going to a Buddhist center. She's learning to meditate. She says it will **help her have a peaceful mind**. It must be working, because she stays peaceful even when she catches me tossing my baseball inside!

Chapter Four

Giving Thanks

When Dad gets home, he comes to tell me good night. He listens while I say my prayers. I believe God is listening too.

I give thanks for my full stomach. I give thanks for the people I know: Dad, Mom, Zach, Sophia, Fahmi, and Kate. And then, **I give thanks for baseball!**

Make a "How I Can Help" List

Many religions encourage their followers to help other people. People who do not follow a religion often make a point to help others too. What are some ways you could do this? Talk with your family. Then make a list of how your family might work together to be helpers. Here are some ideas to get you started:

1) Do chores for a neighbor or family member who is elderly.

2) Volunteer for an organization that helps people.

3) Clean up your local park.

4) Donate to a food shelf.

5) Give your unneeded items to a charity.

6) Make a card for someone who is sick.

7) Visit a residence for elderly people.

What else can you think of?

GLOSSARY

bar mitzvah: a special celebration when a Jewish boy turns thirteen

bat mitzvah: a special celebration when a Jewish girl turns twelve or thirteen

Buddhism: a way of living based on the teachings of Buddha

Christianity: a religion based on the teachings of Jesus Christ

Eid al-Fitr: a Muslim holiday

Jewish: related to the religion called Judaism or to the people known as Jews

kippah: a small cap worn by Jewish men and some women for prayer

meditate: to focus and calm the mind

Muslim: a follower of Islam, the religion revealed by the Prophet Muhammad

Ramadan: the ninth month of the Islamic calendar

religion: a system of faith and worship

synagogue: a place where Jewish people meet for worship

volunteer: to do something helpful without being paid

worship: to show honor and devotion to a god or gods

BOOKS

Blanchard, Eliza. *A Child's Book of Blessings and Prayers*. Boston: Skinner House Books, 2008. Read this book to discover prayers and blessings that come from different religious traditions.

Kalman, Bobbie. *What Is Religion?* New York: Crabtree, 2009. This book will help you learn more about the beliefs and practices of different world religions.

Rotner, Shelley, and Sheila M. Kelly. *Many Ways: How Families Practice Their Beliefs and Religions*. Minneapolis: Millbrook, 2006. Simple text and colorful photos show how children from around the world practice their religious beliefs.

WEBSITES

World Religions Homework Help
http://www.primaryhomeworkhelp.co.uk/Religion.html
Visit this website with your family to learn more about some of the world's major religions.

Zoom into Action: Family Guide to Volunteering
http://www-tc.pbskids.org/zoom/grownups/action/pdfs/volunteer_guide.pdf
Read this helpful guide from PBS Kids with your family to learn more about how you can become volunteers and help people.

LERNER *e* SOURCE™
Expand learning beyond the printed book. Download free, complementary educational resources for this book from our website, www.lerneresource.com.